Big Bunnies
and Little Chicks

 A GOLDEN BOOK®
Western Publishing Company, Inc.
Racine, Wisconsin 53404
No part of this book may be reproduced or copied without
® written permission from the publisher. Produced in U.S.A.

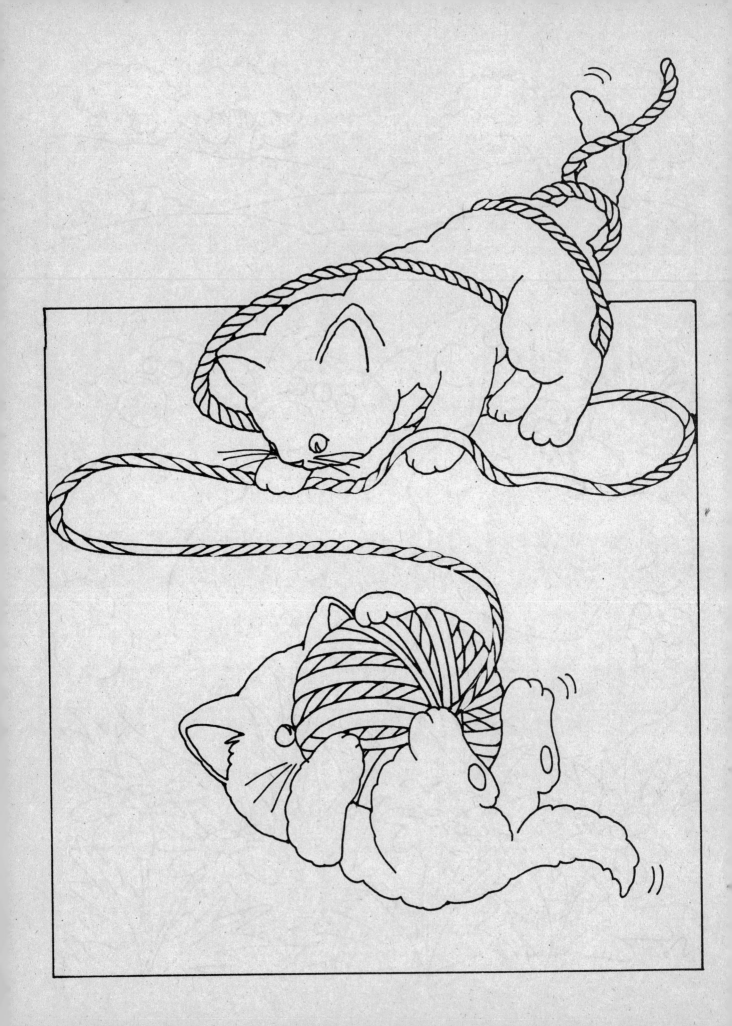

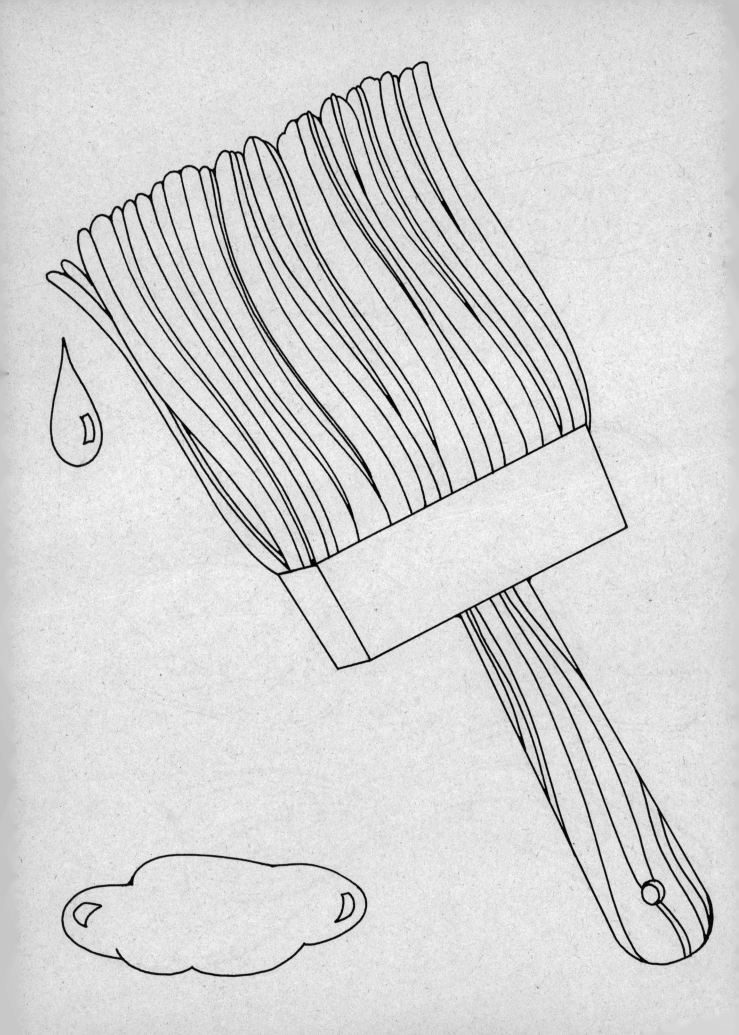

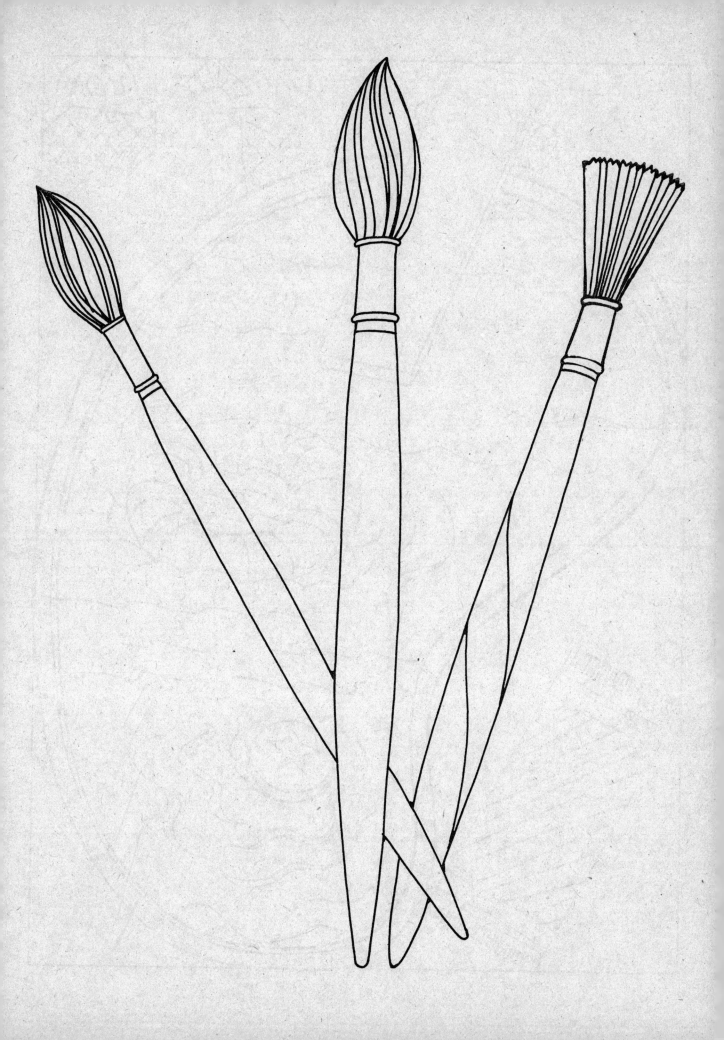

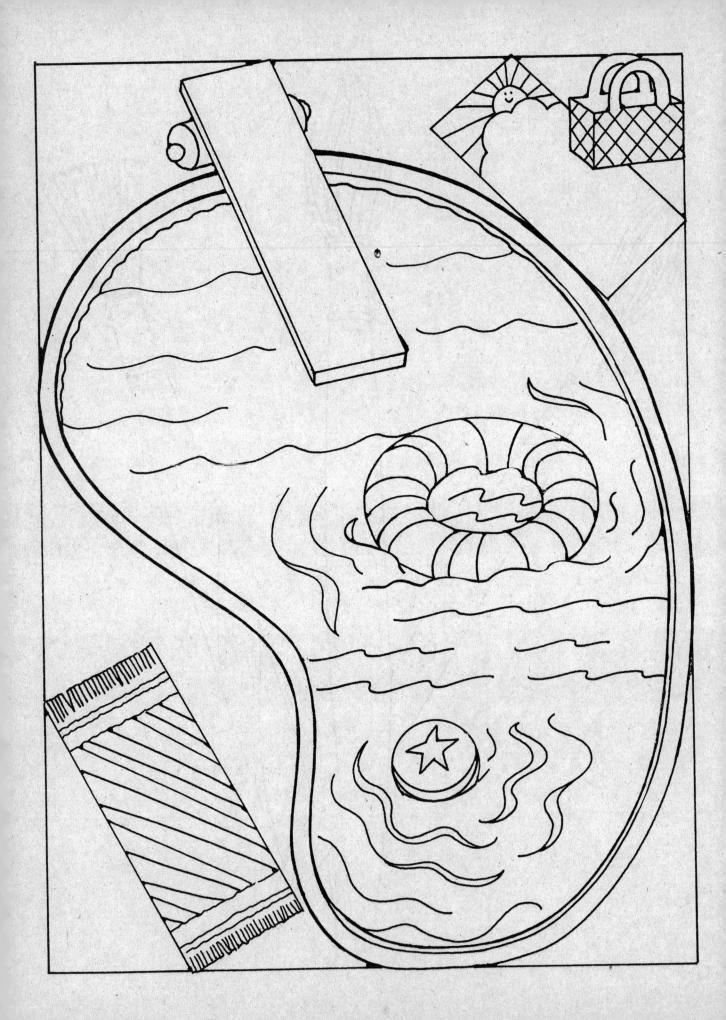

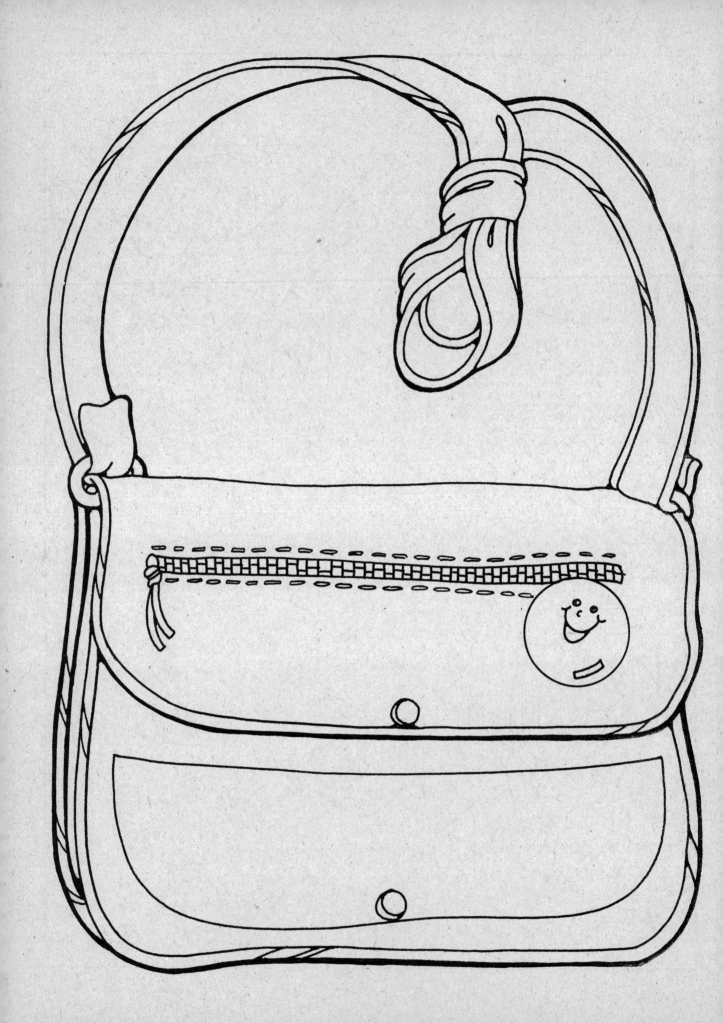